VENUS ANH

This paperback edition published in 2017

Copyright ©2017 MLSund

Edited by Claire Wingfield

Published by SSL Publishing, Canada

English language paperback
ISBN: 978-0-9959133-0-1

Cover photograph by MLSund
Taken at Pompeii.

Visit
venusanh.com
for a full list of credits
and more content.

The "VA" symbol is a registered design trademark.

For Anh

Introduction

This work of fiction, set in ancient Rome, interlaces the imaginary lives of mythical characters invented by the author amidst those of real historical public figures and a few divine beings as well. Although written as an autobiography, it surely is not. With the exception of the known public figures, any resemblance of characters to persons living or dead is coincidental and unintended.

Many of the events and their respective locations referenced in this story are aimed at being historically accurate. To the extent this has been achieved, the author is indebted to those who produced the insightful publications and material listed in the acknowledgements.

Knowing art is detail perfectly placed, the author has attempted to interject the fictional characters into available spaces amongst the swirling set of famous figures that largely defined the late Roman Republic. In some situations, the invented characters pull and stretch certain truths, breathe life into rumours, and embellish facts. Even the real beings are given to utter statements that they probably never said. It is therefore highly advisable that the reader of this tale never relies on anything here as fact; it is hoped instead that this epic piques her curiosity in all things Roman, and prompts her to delve into proper historical references.

This story, of course, speaks about more than just Roman history; it weaves a mystical journey through topics of women's rights, leadership, power and influence, commitment and deceit, relationships and sexuality, rage and revenge, divinity and the abyss. Complementary material on this story is available at the website venusanh.com.

Scene I
111 BC

I, Venus Anh of Rome,
Born at my Bithynian home
On 21 April 100 BC,
Descend from my father,
Nicomedes IV,
The region's final king,
And from my mother,
Anh,
An Asian woman from distant East
Who travelled an epic journey
Across sea and sand
Eleven years before my birth,
Having fled the first Chinese invasion
Of her home in Vietnam.

Mother Anh
From a farm
In Thanh Hóa Province
Near a great river,
Sông Mã,
Witnessed her father's slaughter
At a rice field
By Chinese invaders.
His body was taken
By the invaders
And thrown to the sea.
Mother Anh managed to escape
With her farm slave master,

Quyen,
Master Quyen.
Being a man of slight build,
Yet of great ability and strength,
He was a man
Filled with compassion
For Mother Anh
And all women
And all men.

Mother Anh
And Master Quyen
Thieved a small sturdy vessel,
A Chinese junk,
Moored at Sông Mã
And escaped on an epic journey
Southward and westward.
They knew not their destination,
But it was far from slaughterers
They hoped.

Their route at sea
Never veered beyond sight of coastal lands,
For neither traveller had experience
In navigating open waters,
And they feared the edge of the earth
Awaited them just beyond the ocean's horizon.

Scene II
111 BC

Months later,
They reached a place in Arabia
At the edge of endless sands
Near a city called Gerrha
Where Master Quyen's death at sea
Came at the swords of Parthian warriors
Who stormed their weathered vessel.

The warriors,
Savages they were,
Severed Master Quyen's head,
Believing he was too old
To be a useful slave,
And dumped his remains to sea.
They dragged Mother Anh
Across the boat's blood-drenched planks
And wrenched her to shore
Through burning hot winds.
The crew of a merchant vessel
Bound Mother Anh
In tightly-cinched ropes,
Then heaved her aboard.
They set sail
Along the arid sea shore
Until they came upon
The mouth of a great river,
The river Euphrates,
Up which they continued

Their sluggish journey
Until reaching the town of Borsippa.
In the centre of that town of trade
On the riverbank
Mother Anh
Felt swallowed up
And smothered
Within the crowded and chaotic streets,
Submerged in hot dust-filled air.

Mother Anh,
Many years later,
Learnt that this town
Dwelled in the shadows
Of the splintered walls of Babylon,
A decimated city
Brought down upon judgement
Of its fornications.
It was said
The sand and soil
At Babylon,
So tainted by evil doings,
Did spread tarnished spirits
To all surrounding lands
Touched by the Euphrates,
Causing all its wise men
To perish
And all its good inhabitants to flee.
And so Mother Anh told me later in her life:
"My fortunes and fate, cursed I fear,
Having pressed my feet
Into those poisoned sands."

Scene III
111 BC

There in Borsippa
Beneath the ziggurat,
Mother Anh's masters
Chained her to a table,
Requiring her to slave
In a bronze and iron workshop,
Making swords of the same design
As that used to sever Master Quyen.
Mother Anh worked alongside
Another slave from Vietnam,
A young man with great energy and character.
He wore deep scars upon his face, arms and back,
And a patch that concealed his gorged eye.
He had acquired some knowledge
Of the Parthian language
Spoken by his masters,
And the young man interpreted their commands
For Mother Anh.
Her torturous labour
And thoughts of Master Quyen
Broke Mother Anh's heart every day.
When she wept,
Her slave masters delivered lashes across her back,
While reminding her: "No tears are permitted
In this place of beautiful swords."

Scene IV
111 BC

Mother Anh,
Scheming her escape,
Believed the only way out
Was to sell her body
To a traitor
Who promised
To break her free
One dark night
From the prison workshop
And transport her further west
To a new life in a prosperous kingdom.
The traitor was her guard by day,
A man whose eyes
Were dark and empty,
And whose heart seemed filled
With stone and sand.

After surrendering her body
To the guard
One horrid night,
Mother Anh thought
She had sealed her escape.
Yet, one spate of sex
Was not enough
For the guard
Who demanded twelve more
Nights of violation.
Mother Anh

Persevered
Somehow.
Mother Anh,
Battered,
Bruised
And bloodied.

She explained to me years later:
"I chose to battle through
Nearly a fortnight in the deepest hell,
For what cause?
My dear,
One shall never pay
A devil's toll
Unless it surely casts him aside
And clears the path
To one's noble goal."

Mother Anh
Fell into a heap of exhausted relief
On the night of her escape.
By horse and carriage
The guard set out with Mother Anh
On a journey of 33 days' duration
Over a distance of 1089 Royal Miles
Westward along the Royal Road,
A congested route
Packed with travellers of every description.
Upon approach to the route's terminus
At the city of Sardis,
Mother Anh and the guard turned northward
Towards the kingdom of Bithynia,
A fertile land of promise.

Scene V
111 BC

On a fateful evening
Lit by dangling crescent moon
That somehow symbolised
That murky land,
Mother Anh
And the guard
Arrived near the city of Nicomedia
At a forested area
Beside an ocean bay.
They were met by an agent,
A dark-bearded man
With cloth upon his head
Who paid the guard one gold coin
In exchange for the slave,
Mother Anh.
The guard released her
From binding chains.
Mother Anh
Then turned to the guard
Who had ably transported her
And completed the contract
The only way she would;
By withdrawing a dagger
From under her cloak,
A dagger she'd crafted
So finely
For this occasion
And delivered it

With all her might
Straight through his heart,
Ending her blight.
Yet, a single thrust
Not enough;
Twelve more
Seemed a fitting score.

At full tilt
The agent took the horse from the carriage
And dashed into the night.
Mother Anh
Clenched the gold coin
That had fallen onto the leafy pathway
And dragged the guard's
Blood-stained body
To the seashore
And laid it there,
But not in the water.
"Only the worthy
Should die at sea,"
She thought.

Scene VI
111 BC

Mother Anh
Returned to the carriage
And laid down to rest.
With her head upon
The wooden planks
She recalled the terrifying moments
On the deck of the junk
And her epic journey.

Her first night in Bithynia
Was not one of sleep
But rather of
A thousand thoughts and dreams,
Doubts and regrets,
Fears and questions.
Yet pleasant thoughts
Of Master Quyen
Drifted through her head.
"A great man," she thought,
"But why?
Just a farmer!
Wearing splashes of mud and soil,
What knowledge could come from hardship and toil?"
His piercing eyes,
With intense look of concentration
Locked and engaged
The listener when he spoke:
"My name Quyen means 'powerful'.

My father taught me
That man has power,
But it's useless if misdirected.
Thus, man shall consult
With the calm foresight of his good wife,
Else he is sure to veer off-course
Or suffer unintended consequences
Of his strengths misapplied."

He continued:
"A man has the power
To control,
Even choke his wife,
But this is suicide,
Stifling the one
Who brings him stability.
I was taught:
Free the woman at your side.
You need her uninhibited thoughts.
Tell her what Confucius said:
I want you to be everything that's you,
Deep at the centre of your being."

Master Quyen concluded:
"Even the strongest man
Cannot carry his community alone.
It is the loving couple,
Bound as equals,
That is the smallest stable building block
Upon which to construct
A virtuous society."

Mother Anh
Began to understand

Why Master Quyen
Had not beaten her
Or abused her
As his slave.
Master Quyen
Revealed his need for a wife,
Yet had none.
He relied
On Mother Anh's guidance,
And she, in turn,
Gained deep wisdom
From the great Master Quyen.
Mother Anh felt comforted
As she contemplated her value as a woman.

Sleep finally overcame her
Late that night
Under a blanket
Of heavy summer air.

Scene VII
111 BC

At sunrise
Mother Anh was awoken in the carriage
By a large man
Looming over her.
She grabbed her dagger,
Still blood-stained.
"I am your new master,
Master Elpidius," said the man.
His voice was calming to Mother Anh,
Although she could not comprehend
The Latin language he spoke.
"It sounded like rocks tumbling in a stream,"
She told me on one occasion.

Master Elpidius
Donned a white robe
And red Phrygian cap,
A symbol of a liberated slave,
Which seemed a peculiar choice of garb
For a slave master.
He was an ironsmith and sword maker,
One of great reputation and skill,
A craftsman of the highest order,
Known to the local royal family
For his prized hardware.
He had plans
For Mother Anh,
Having been apprised

Of her aptitude
In the art of ironsmithing.

Master Elpidius
Secured Mother Anh
Upon a padded seat
Within the bed of his carriage,
Then drove to his workshop near a bay.
Along the way,
Mother Anh said a prayer:
"Though tied and bound so tightly by these ropes
On Tuesday's sunrise washed in golden light,
This day I pray to God that all my hopes
Will be achieved without continued fight."

Scene VIII
111 BC

Master Elpidius
Was a Roman man of few words,
Though he was a teacher.
He tutored Mother Anh
In the art of speaking and reading
Greek and Latin languages,
And Mother Anh
Recognized what a rare gift
He bestowed to a slave.

Master Elpidius,
Keeping more than 20 slaves,
Was head craftsman in his workshop.
He led his workers by example,
Keeping production rates high
While tending to details
And ever increasing quality.
He was patient
Most of the time.
When he saw unique talents
In any of the slaves,
And a good work ethic,
He praised and promoted,
Even allowing some
Life-affirming creativity
To be incorporated
In the designs of his impeccable hardware.

But Master Elpidius
Demanded vigorous work;
Should a slave fail to produce,
Or dissent,
The heat of his temper
Was at times unguarded.
Mother Anh witnessed
Harsh words, beatings and torture
Of some of her fellow slaves.
On one occasion Master Elpidius
Removed the hands of a slave
With a single strike of his sword.
He had learnt this method of punishment
As a Roman warrior
In years gone by.

Mother Anh spoke to Master Elpidius:
"I beg of you, my master,
To consider before unleashing fire
At a slave,
That he may suffer
Some physical ailment
Or mental incapacity.
Perhaps he wants to please you
But is unable.
Perhaps he even loves you.
If you desire
To thrash a slave,
Tell of your anger first to me.
Let me listen to you
In closed quarters.
Then, following the next sunrise,
Consider your response
And go forward to the slave.

I beg of you, my master."
Master Elpidius
Dismissed Mother Anh's request,
But his face showed consideration.

A short time later,
He came to her.
He spoke of frustration.
Unhappiness.
Anger with some slaves
And even with his mistresses.
There were many anxieties
Behind the great man.
Over time, he opened
To Mother Anh
More frequently.
His impulsive outbursts diminished.
And his punishment of slaves became quieter,
Yet more effective.
They grew fonder of him, and did not wish to disappoint.
Eventually,
Mother Anh did not witness
Another slave beating
At the hands of Master Elpidius.

Scene IX
101 BC

For ten years,
Master Elpidius
Continually trained and mentored
Mother Anh.
Being so impressed
By her dedication and talent,
He promoted her
To the status of *prima ancilla*.
She continued crafting
Ever more beautiful works
In iron, bronze and leather,
Fashioning all varieties of
Swords, armour and shields,
Helmets, ensigns and standards.
Even trumpets and drums.
Mother Anh became a skilled artisan
Whose reputation spread far and wide
Throughout the kingdom.

In the year 101 BC, a scroll was delivered
By a royal messenger to Master Elpidius.
It was a note
Written in the hand of
Nicomedes III, king of Bithynia,
Ordering the creation
Of a grand set of armour for himself.
It was to be decorated
With intricate paintings,

Silver and gold inlays,
And gems
Including emeralds, rubies and diamonds.
This grand royal set
Was to be presented to him
At his palace by the sea
During a royal ceremony and feast
In the month of May.
Master Elpidius and Mother Anh
Were invited guests.

Mother Anh
Worked diligently
Day and night,
Crafting the finest set
For the king.
All slaves assisted her
In the workshop
And Master Elpidius
Was delighted with the final result,
A masterpiece,
A royal treasure,
Created by Mother Anh.

Scene X
101 BC

Just after sunrise
On the day of the royal ceremony,
Roman soldiers came to the workshop
To collect the royal set of armour.
By late afternoon,
Mother Anh, not at ease,
Attended the ceremony
With Master Elpidius.
Uncaring for riches, excess and royalty,
Mother Anh wished not to dwell
At the royal palace,
A place of no joy for her,
But for meeting the king's son,
Nicomedes.
His impressive physical stature
And strong sculpted face
Lured Mother Anh's glance,
Met by Nicomedes' smile,
And a momentous bond
Began that night.

Scene XI
101 BC

Months later,
During a hot and still summer evening,
With countless glittering stars
Filling the sky,
The royal messenger
Arrived once again at the workshop
To deliver a scroll,
This time wrapping a single, thorn-less red rose.
The royal messenger
Handed the scroll to Master Elpidius, who,
Without hesitation,
Passed it to Mother Anh.
She turned as red as the rose
With embarrassment and shyness.
She took the rose
And musingly unrolled the scroll
To reveal a short letter
Written beautifully in the hand
Of Nicomedes, the king's son.
The message was brief: "Your presence
Tomorrow night
At the royal palace
Is requested."
Mother Anh's night at the palace,
She recalled to me,
Seemed an endless lover's night.

Scene XII
100 BC

Upon my birth
In Bithynia on 21 April 100 BC
I was given only one name,
That of my mother,
Anh.
Nicomedes was informed of my birth
And declared:
"My daughter is sent from the gods,
Having been born
On the day
That Romulus set out the markings
Of the great wall
Surrounding Rome,
His new glorious city,
Some 653 years ago."
Nicomedes informed
The Pontifex Maximus in Rome
Of the glorious event of my birth,
Who sent for a Vestal Virgin
To travel from Rome to see me,
To touch me,
Freeing me from slavery,
And to bless me
And to proclaim
That I am a Roman citizen
Of patrician class
And have the ability to speak with gods.

Scene XIII
94 BC

When I was six years of age
My father ascended to the throne
As King Nicomedes IV
Upon the death of his father.
At that time
I was already working as a slave
Alongside Mother Anh
Despite my elevated class
And connection with the gods;
My father did not want my existence
Widely know within the kingdom.
He told Mother Anh: "My standing
Will diminish amongst Bithynians
Should they know
I knelt to the level
Of a far-eastern slave."

Although I toiled in the workshop
For many years,
I was not able to achieve
The level of skill
Realised by Mother Anh,
Nor was I able to achieve
The status of *prima ancilla.*
Yet I worked faithfully
With all my strength.

Working with Mother Anh

Was a blessing for me;
She shared her vast knowledge and wisdom
Gained through her own experiences
And those of the great
Master Quyen.

On my fourteenth birthday
Mother Anh gave me her dagger
And gold coin.
She told me: "Keep these close to you.
They brought me protection and favour.
Bless you Anh, I wish you safety and freedom."
I felt empowered.
Yet, as years of painstaking labour passed,
Doubt set into my thoughts:
"Who am I?
What is my role?
Value?
Future?
Why am I here?
I am of patrician class!
I can speak with gods!
Shall I slit the throat of my Master
And free Mother Anh,
All the slaves
And myself?"
I subdued these dire thoughts
And continued to work,
In pain.

Scene XIV
80 BC

When I was 20 years old
And Mother Anh almost 50,
The royal messenger
Once again appeared at the workshop,
Looking aged,
But of comforting and familiar sight.
He delivered a scroll
To Master Elpidius
That ordered me to the royal palace.
The reason was not divulged.
I was gleeful
Until Mother Anh explained to me
Perchance I was to marry Nicomedes IV,
My own father.
She speculated
This would strengthen his bond with Rome,
His kingdom's favoured ally.
I dreaded this thought
Of incestuous marriage
But felt my conviction
To a greater fulfilment of service
Beyond my person.
I was proud
To think that I might
Contribute to the peace and stability
Of our kingdom.

I was taken the following afternoon

In an historic preserved golden chariot
By a Roman soldier,
Accompanied by four others on horseback,
To the royal palace
Where a large gathering of Romans,
Including senators,
Crowded the grand chamber.
But I was not to be seen.
I was sneaked
Through a concealed back door
To a candle-lit hallway
And up a narrow dark staircase
Of cold grey stone
Where, at the top, my father stood,
Looking down at me.

He took my hand, with no word said
And led me, shaking in fear,
To his room's giant bed.
He seated me there
Beside a table
With lace and silk garments on top,
And said to me:
"A guest arrives here tonight,
A young Roman leader,
One whom I believe will be
Bithynia's future king.
My gift to him is you,
A Bithynian treasure for Rome.
Give him all he seeks in pleasure
As your mother gave me."
I fainted in relief and joy.

When I awoke

There was only silence
And stillness.
I was lying on the king's bed.
I sensed motion in the room
And peered to the side.
A man in a purple silk robe
Was lounging on a golden sofa.
I lurched and yelped in surprise.
The man,
A young, noble-looking man
Stood and walked quietly to me
And said in a soft boyish voice:
"Fear not, I am here to keep you.
I have travelled from Rome
To retrieve a fleet,
But that work is now complete,
And I remain in Bithynia
Because I know of your presence.
I am Gaius Julius Caesar,
A Roman citizen
And a descendant of the goddess Venus
Who knows of your birth and life."

I asked: "Who is this goddess?"
Caesar responded: "She will speak to you.
And you will follow her
At a later time.
But tonight is ours."

At that moment
A lady peered around the bedroom door
And said to me: "I am Nysa, your father's sister.
I will assist to robe you
In these laces and silks

For your gentleman's delight."
Caesar left the room
And Nysa removed my clothing.
She fitted me in the laces and silks
While caressing me lightly
Over the length of my body.
She asked me to lie on the bed,
As she continued touching me,
Arousing me.
I felt a pulsing desire
Throbbing within me,
One like I had never known.
Caesar returned to the room
And said: "Now is your time
To taste the pleasures of Rome
That are, surely, incomparable."

Scene XV
80 BC

That night of pleasure
Turned to days and weeks,
As I remained in the royal palace.
Caesar departed each day,
Tending to business with merchants and clients,
And returned to me each night
In our chamber of love.

One morning
Caesar told me he must leave Bithynia
For other duties,
So upon his departure
I returned to my home,
To Mother Anh at the workshop.
She looked weak and tired
But blissful to see me.
I resumed my work,
Unsure,
More than ever,
What my destiny would be.

Just a few days later,
Master Elpidius informed me
I was to return to the royal palace
To be with Caesar again.
I embraced Caesar in our secluded suite
And he took me upon the bed
And held me

And looked down at me
Deep into my eyes
And said:
"I am sending you to Rome
And there you shall be cared for
And you will find your place
Amongst the Romans.
I cannot accompany you now,
But I shall join you in haste
When my work is complete."

Scene XVI
80 BC

My first taste of life in Rome,
The glorious city of Romulus,
Was a delightful treat of sweet honey.
I saw glorious structures and monuments
That only giants, nay gods
Could sculpt so finely
And lift skyward.
They framed the city streets and squares
That teemed with crowds of people
Of diverse classes and origins.
Apparently a chaotic mix,
Yet collectively achieving the highest society.
As I navigated through the rivers of the populace
That streamed through the cobbled alleys
I felt respected by all.
I felt patrician for the first time.

Caesar's home was located
In the crude Suburra area,
Bestrewn with plebeians and prostitutes.
But it was a palace to me.
I was happy to reside there
With Caesar's wife, Cornelia,
Who occupied separate quarters
With their daughter, Julia.
Cornelia was kind to me;
We helped each other.
I cared for Julia while Cornelia tended chores.

Cornelia and I gave love to each other,
Very deep and passionate love,
During Caesar's extended absence.

Cornelia disclosed to me: "The true reason
Caesar has fled Rome
Is to escape arrest
And execution
By Rome's dictator,
Lucius Cornelius Sulla.
He demanded
That Caesar divorce me,
Because my father was one of his enemies.
Caesar refuses to leave me."

The following day
I called upon the Vestal Virgin
Who touched me at Bithynia.
I beseeched her to convince Sulla
To pardon Caesar.
The Vestal Virgin agreed to meet Sulla,
Taking with her Caesar's mother, Aurelia.
By the following week
Sulla announced his pardon of Caesar
And even his intention to relinquish his dictatorship.
I knew not how the Vestal Virgin achieved this
Unlikely feat, and rumours circulated
That the Vestal Virgin
Had bribed Sulla with favours.
Nonetheless,
Cornelia and I celebrated together,
For we knew
Our Caesar was coming home.

Scene XVII
79 BC

I walked to the Forum one afternoon
And came upon a group of men
Who silenced their chatter as I approached
And turned to me with smiles.
"Is the Queen of Bithynia here?" one man asked.
I explained: "No, I am not yet queen,
Although daughter of Nicomedes IV."
"No my lady, I speak of Julius Caesar,"
Replied the man.
"I do not understand," I said.
Another man offered:
"Caesar lingered in your father's suite
What was his task? Washing the king's feet?
Queen of Bithynia is how Caesar is known
The king wanted joys from the boy that he owned.
Now all of Rome
Knows Caesar's vice;
He pleasured the king
Without thinking twice."

Without reply,
I strode away,
Realising what horrible rumour had spread.
I considered what actions to take
But none were needed.
For the truth is absolute, without excuse.
Caesar's love for me was truth.

Scene XVIII
79 BC

Cornelia and I were overjoyed
The day our Caesar arrived home.
He was exhausted.
He had battled in a triumphant war
At the city of Mytilene,
Where his heroic actions in saving a soldier's life
Had earned him the *corona civica*,
The wreath of oak leaves upon his head
Symbolising Rome's highest military honour.

After days of rest
With relaxing baths
And massages by servants,
Caesar was fresh and energised.
He was blissful in the comfort of his home,
Playing with his young daughter
And sipping Retsina he'd brought from Greece.
During the latest night hours,
Cornelia and Caesar and I
Pleasured one another
While taking turns
Wearing the *corona civica*.

Scene XIX
78 BC

One evening
A lady with a young boy
Visited our home.
Cornelia introduced the lady to me:
"This is Servilia."
I enquired: "And this her son?"
Cornelia replied: "Yes, his name is
Marcus Junius Brutus."
I smiled at the cute boy,
Who had an eye twinkle for me.
He was brought to see his "sister Julia,"
Said Servilia.
Cornelia turned to me,
And explained: "Caesar is Brutus' father,
And Servilia his mother."
This revelation, a shock that sank my heart,
Induced woeful thoughts: "How many lovers
Does my Caesar have?
And how many children?"
Servilia said to Cornelia:
"We shall speak later, alone,"
And leaned closer to her,
Adding in hushed tone:
"So this is the Anh?
Dame of slave and king?
Who bewitched Caesar,
Yet gives him nothing?"

Scene XX
75 BC

One quiet afternoon
Caesar gathered Cornelia and I
To inform us that he would travel to Rhodes
To study with a well-reputed teacher of oratory.
He then said to me: "I must
Address an important matter with you
In confidence prior to my journey."

A few days later,
Caesar took me
To the Temple of Concord at the Forum
After the senators had retired
To their afternoon baths.
Caesar left me alone
In a small library room in the temple.
Moments later,
I heard a voice
Which seemed to come
From behind a stack of scrolls,
But nobody was there.
"Follow your angels," the voice whispered.
I was fearful but curious.
"What angels?" I asked.
"They watch over you," was the reply.
At that moment
I was uncomfortable
Without my Caesar.
I dashed out of the temple,

Down the wide marble staircase
And into the Forum.
It seemed unusually peaceful
For that time of day
In the centre of Rome.

I came upon four ladies
Who were standing and talking.
They silenced as I approached,
And turned to me, smiling.
One spoke: "Someone awaits you!
Come with us to the river."
I asked: "Is it my Caesar?"
The second lady replied:
"No, but he guides you."
I enquired further: "To what place?"
The third lady said: "It is not a place,
But a passage of fate."
I responded: "His guidance is my current."
The ladies walked with me
From the Forum
To a small boat
Moored at the shore of the Tiber
Adjacent to the river island.
The fourth lady spoke:
"Dearest Anh, your journey begins aboard
This vessel, so readied to take you to
The beginning of your destiny. Lord
Be your guide who doth prepare and keep you."

Fear struck me;
My body cinched with tension
As my memory flashed
With vivid image

Of Mother Anh's journey at sea,
And its horrid ending.
Nonetheless I stepped aboard
The small boat.
I assured myself
That I was strong;
I gripped tightly
My dagger for protection
And my gold coin for luck.
Alone, I drifted quietly down the river
To its terminus where it's consumed
By the vast sea,
At which point
I landed at the shore
And walked up the sandy beach
With lush trees beside.
After some time
I sat in warm sunlight,
Against a large rock,
And fell into a dreamy sleep.

I awoke to the sound
Of a lovely female voice:
"Hello."
I wondered: "A voice from where?"
I turned and there she was.
I knew, without any doubt,
With red hair and hazel eyes,
Nude and natural,
From the sea,
Venus, goddess of love.
Goddess of beauty and sex,
Of fertility and desire,
Of prosperity and victory.

My goddess,
From whom my Caesar descended.
"What have you learnt
Of woman and the world?"
Asked my goddess.

We sat for hours
Together,
Embracing,
Talking of my experiences
And those of Mother Anh.
My goddess enquired:
"What does woman contribute?
And what enables her?"
I contemplated, and replied:
"When unrestrained, we can calm waves.
I also ask myself,
What conflict a woman can prevent
When minding her man?
What wars were started by women?"

My goddess spoke: "Anh,
I give you your *praenomen*,
Venus.
Henceforth,
You will be known as
Venus Anh."

Then, my goddess
Revealed to me:
"Venus Anh,
You shall take these truths
And disseminate them:

"Iura feminae universa infinitaque
securitatis
libertatis
aequalitatis
et officia feminae universa infinitaque
ductus
ministerii
amoris.

"Woman's universal and infinite rights of
Security,
Liberty,
Equality,
And woman's universal and infinite duties of
Leadership,
Service,
Love."

My goddess continued:
"These truths shall be known
As the Tables of the Venus Anh.
Let it be known
Man can veer guideless without woman,
Albeit with strength,
And woman can fall short of power without man,
Albeit with compassion.
Only when entwined,
Strongly bound,
And of equal influence,
Can they together advance societies.
All kings and leaders,
All men,
Who free women with their rights
To deliver their duties

46

Will advance their societies.
Those who do not
Will stagnate
And suffer
In perpetual war and misery.
Such is seen through the eye of providence
Of our Egyptian goddess Isis
Who watches over us as protectorate
And who recites and affirms:
'Femina ac vir una conficientes.'
Woman and man, together achieving."

At that moment
My goddess Venus gave me a white seashell
Inscribed with three markings on each side
Representing three rights and three duties
Of the Tables of the Venus Anh.

I held the shell
To my bare chest
And laid in the arms
Of my goddess
And we slept in the sun
Until the sound of waves awoke me.
At such time I rose from the sand
With shell in hand
And my goddess Venus
Had slipped from sight.

Scene XXI
75 BC

I returned to my boat
Where two Roman soldiers
Were waiting
To take me home.
During my journey back,
I was still in a dreamy state of mind,
Feeling safe and secure,
And only realized after reaching Rome
That I had forgotten my gold coin and dagger,
Left behind at the beach.
Thankfully, however, I retained my sacred shell.

When I walked through the Forum
The four ladies again appeared.
I stood before them
And a small crowd gathered around us.
I proclaimed:
"Our goddess Venus revealed to me
At the beach at Ostia
The Tables of the Venus Anh:
Woman's universal and infinite rights of
Security,
Liberty,
Equality,
And woman's universal and infinite duties of
Leadership,
Service,
Love."

The gathered people
Heard my message
And a girl asked:
"These are truths?"
And I said: "All people who follow
The Tables of the Venus Anh
Will achieve great societies and will prosper.
All those who dismiss these truths
Shall choke in the dust and sand
Of perpetual war and misery."

I held the sacred shell to my chest,
And told all those who had gathered:
"This is the sacred shell
Of the Venus Anh.
Upon each side,
Three markings
Symbolising three rights
And three duties."

"O, mankind!
Venus hath mercy," a lady said.

Upon my return to Caesar that day,
Without a word spoken,
He knew I had met our goddess Venus
And that I had received
The Tables of the Venus Anh.

Scene XXII
74 BC

Caesar departed for Rhodes
And I was uneasy,
Fearing for his safety.
There was a day
When black birds
Descended all around our home
With no apparent cause.
I called for Cornelia
To witness the eerie sight.
She said:
"This auspice, surely an evil omen.
May Caesar endure!"
As feared, a grievous message
Was soon delivered to us,
Stating that Caesar had been taken hostage
By pirates in the Mediterranean.
I shook my head in disbelief
And suffered unrelenting grief.
Cornelia and I prayed.

Months later,
Another scroll was brought
With message of Caesar's freedom;
He had escaped his captors
And resumed his travels to Rhodes.
Despite our feelings of great relief and joy,
Cornelia and I continued to see birds
Day after day

Around our home,
But not in other parts of Rome.

Yet again, a note delivered,
My breath held and body quivered.
I called for Cornelia
And we read together:
"With regrets from Bithynia,
Nicomedes IV and Mother Anh
Were found stabbed to death
In the king's bed.
The invader, the murderer,
Escaped by horse and carriage.
He shall face his sentence
Of death by crucifixion
When captured.
Upon discovery of the crime,
We the Bithynian guards
Duly called Elpidius,
Artisan of royal armoury,
To witness the bodies.
We pray for your safety,
Venus Anh,
And that of all Romans,
And hereby issue a forewarning
In case this wicked character
Spreads his terror
Elsewhere in the Republic."

I sank for one year
In sadness and sorrow,
Concealing my fear
Beneath blankets of woe.

Scene XXIII
73 BC

The following year
Cornelia and I
Were overjoyed
When our Caesar
Returned to Rome.
He had completed his studies at Rhodes
And, unsurprisingly,
Even led a successful battle
Against enemy forces in Asia
During his study period.

Caesar was called to join
The college of pontiffs,
Rome's elite priesthood,
A highest honour
For our love, defender of Rome.
And he began consulting with me
On many issues.
He was most proud of his military successes
But was not at ease about his desire
To see the enemy's blood.
He confided in me
That he secretly admired
The brutality of military triumphs
By one of his idols, Gnaeus Pompeius Magnus,
Known admiringly as Pompey the Great,
A pre-eminent young Roman general.
Caesar wanted to emulate

Pompey's arrogant successes,
Punctuated with cruelty and gore.
Caesar craved
To similarly crush his enemies,
To punish them,
To make them suffer.
He knew it was not justified
And was, at times, privately overcome
With self-doubt.
So he asked me
If he was a good leader,
A good defender of Rome,
A good person.
I said to Caesar:
"It is a gallant pursuit to defend Rome,
But to limit infliction of wound
To that required.
Pompey has no proper woman to guide him
And is devoid of a balancing force.
Caesar, your victories are for the Romans,
Not for your personal gratification."
He reflected
And later confided:
"We must battle
To defend our *magnifica societas*.
But how?
Man's battle methods
Must be justifiable
When placed in the crucible
Of cross-examination,
Not only by his male peers
But also in the presence of woman."

Scene XXIV
70 BC

Several years passed
When, at the age of 30,
Caesar was first eligible
To hold office of quaestorship.
As the election date approached,
He began canvassing in Rome
As a young aristocrat,
Wearing his *toga candidus* in the Forum,
Showily,
A brilliant white toga
To attract voters' attention.

I met Caesar one afternoon
In the Forum
While he was surrounded
By many citizens,
Future voters,
Listening.
He seduced them
With his charm and knowledge,
His confidence and quiet strength.
And when Caesar saw me
He turned his attention to me,
Putting me above others,
As he did many times.
At that moment
A messenger in the Forum declared:
"The senators wish to deliver a message

To all citizens and peoples
At the Rostrum
And request all to attend forthwith."
As the crowds filed away
Caesar remained with me, alone
On a vacated street
And held me lovingly while speaking:
"These senators think highly
Of their grand announcements.
Let them fill the air with trivial tones;
It gives me a moment to touch your sweet skin."
We stood and kissed.
As I consumed his wanting lips,
A shadow moved across me
Blocking the intense mid-day sun.
A figure in dark robe
Stood beside Caesar.
"Witness what I found,"
The man said,
Opening the palm of his hand,
Revealing a gold coin,
The coin I had forgotten at the beach.
The coin Mother Anh took at Bithynia.
The coin that fell to the parched ground.
My eyes
Travelled up from the coin
Along the man's arm,
To his face
Covered with dark beard,
And head wrapped in cloth.
I knew it was the agent
Sent years ago
To buy a slave: Mother Anh.

He smiled
With evil wince
And said to me:
"This coin is mine,
Paid to my brother,
Who was laid slain
Upon its receipt.
How did you come to hold it?"
I replied:
"Your knowledge
Is not hidden,
Your knowledge that
This coin
Paid to a traitor
Was earned by the confinement
And rape of Mother Anh,
And was ill-gotten."

The agent responded:
"My business is none of yours.
I support my family,
Earn my keep
And fulfil my duties, justly.
Interference,
I'll have none of.
I am Abdeimos, a Parthian.
Your mother wronged me
And my brother,
And I set it straight.
Now I am here in Rome
To recover what is mine
And to repay debts
And return favours."

I explained:
"You earn your keep
By perpetuating evils
Against women.
Bought and sold,
Slaves, behold.
Raped and battered,
Alas, disposed.
These violations
Of the Tables of the Venus Anh
Secure your demise.
Your actions are not worthy of payment."

Abdeimos,
Now of wicked stare,
Replied: "Men are above women.
Men are in charge of women.
Men rule over women.
Good women know
To remain obedient!"

I proclaimed: "These beliefs
Are fantasies and fallacies
My good man,
The delusions of those who are weak,
Of those lacking intellect,
And blind to the chaos they perpetrate.
For the Tables of the Venus Anh
Proscribe woman's universal and infinite rights of
Security,
Liberty,
Equality.
These are truths
That facilitate

Advancement of societies.
Look beyond the durance
Of your stone walls;
See through the dust in your eyes
And accept truth, though it hurts you so.
Accept the glory of a *magnifica societas*,
One where women and men prosper
In the illumination of these rights.
Let you face the truth
And elevate yourself above the disbelievers
Of the Tables of the Venus Anh
Who wither in oppressive and violent societies
Led by unchecked male hegemony,
Goddess Venus witnesseth."

Abdeimos' rebuttal thrust forth
With great fire:
"You are not to say, woman!
You shall obey your master
And never dissent against man
Else death to you
Venus Anh!"

With that,
Abdeimos reached
For a scabbard concealed under his robe
From which he withdrew a dagger
So familiar in sight;
Mother Anh's dagger,
Given to me,
Forgotten near the sea,
Sharp as razor
Brought to bear
Lunged through my heart

Without a care.
My Caesar braced me
From behind
And lowered me,
Wilted and lifeless.
My blood, a wine-red river,
Given up freely for all,
Gushed onto the cobbled street
And seeped down to the foundations of Rome.

I looked above
At azure sky
Behind cascading columns
And parasol pines.
Four angels appeared overhead
Reaching down for me.
I sensed they were spinning,
Fading.
I heard their voices
Like distant echoes…
One spoken loudest:
"Bless the Venus Anh
And let her see more days."

I soon came to see nothing
And to hear nothing.
I felt as if
I was in a vast and empty space,
In complete darkness,
But someone was listening to me.
That I could speak, I prayed:
"Neither suppression of spirit
Nor subjugation of soul
Possible.

Dear goddess Venus,
Lift me up
By divine ascension,
As truth elevates
Like tides, unstoppable,
This love will last,
It will last forever."

Scene XXV
70 BC

I was floating,
Weightless.
A small band of light
Began to appear.
Clouds formed
Above me,
And below.
All around,
A dreamy glow.
Lying in silence,
I Alone.
Then, from a distance
Through the clouds,
Such a large man approached me
Without sound.
A figure
Donning mounds of curly hair and beard,
Grasping a large object
Which I could not see clearly
Until he neared.
He stood above me
And then I saw
He carried
A serpent-entwined staff.
I was not fearful,
But comforted by this man.
Then, two ladies approached me
From a distance

Through the clouds.
Each lady carried a serpent
Around her neck.
They came to stand each side of me.
I felt at ease and cared for,
Even surrounded by figures unknown.
"I am Aceso,
Goddess of healing," spoke the first lady.
"I am Panacea,
Goddess of universal remedy," spoke the other.
Aceso spoke again:
"Our father, Asklepios,
God of healing,
Delivers you from death.
You shall be healed
By serpent's breath."

Aceso held her serpent up above me
And from its mouth
Came potion thick and smooth
Onto my wound
And across my whole body,
Enveloped
In sensations of ice and snow
To my core,
At first intense,
Then feeling no more.

Then Panacea held her serpent up above me
And from its mouth
Came potion thin and fast
Onto my wound
And across my whole body,
Enveloped

In sensations of ember and fire
To my core,
At first intense,
Then feeling no more.

Asklepios then spoke to me:
"You will sleep tonight
In this holy place,
The abaton at the Temple of Jupiter."

Scene XXVI
70 BC

I awoke
To the sensation of sinking.
I was dropping down
Into hot wind,
Blasting up from a darkened funnel.
Then fire appeared
And the heat and smoke,
Ever increasing,
Engulfed me.
I heard voices,
The voices of many.
Then I saw people standing,
Many people
Shuffling and seeming uneasy,
Like they were waiting for something
Impatiently.
A man behind me shouted:
"Have you come for me?"
I turned to see Abdeimos.
He had been crucified
With blood still seeping from punctures
In his hands and feet.
"What have you done?" I asked him.
"That which was called for," he said.
"By whom?" I asked.
He did not answer.
"Where is your wife?" I asked.
"She died long ago,

And she is in heaven,
I pray" said Abdeimos solemnly.
"We shall pray together," I said.
I held his sticky, blood-stained hand
And we walked through a guarded doorway.
Two shrouded souls
Sealed the black doors behind us
As a great man approached
Wearing two feathers upon his hat.
He gave a *crux ansata* to Abdeimos
Which he held in his right hand.
We closed our eyes
And prayed.
After some time
Abdeimos spoke:
"I, as every man, a disciple,
But of whom?"
That he could hear,
I spoke:
"Go to your wife,
Stay by her side,
Join as equals,
In her soul, abide."

Scene XXVII
70 BC

I rose from cloud
Toward the glow of sunrise,
Goddess Venus my witness,
To see light
And to feel the fresh breeze
At the steps of the Temple of Jupiter.
I wore a brilliant white robe
And I saw a symbol of the Venus Anh
Marked upon my chest
Where the dagger struck through me.

A crowd had gathered,
Waiting and hushed.
A crowd so large
It covered the Capitoline Hill
Upon which the temple rose.
The crowd extended through the Forum
And beyond.
My dear Caesar,
At my side,
Gave me my dagger
Which I raised for all to witness.
And my dear Caesar
Gave me my shell
With three markings upon each side,
Which I took
In my right hand.
I was overwhelmed

By the presence of Romans
And of our goddess Venus
And I was swept into a coronation,
A canonisation,
And I proclaimed to my followers:
"O, dear Romans
And all people,
Our goddess Venus
Revealed to me
At Ostia
The Tables of the Venus Anh,
Which are truths of
Woman's universal and infinite rights of
Security,
Liberty,
Equality,
And of woman's universal and infinite duties of
Leadership,
Service,
Love.
While living these truths,
Woman and man together
Advance societies
And they achieve peace."
I heard my voice carry
Through the sparkling air
To all who stood
In the paradise below the temple,
On Roman streets
Infused with my blood.
I proclaimed, and all recited:
"Femina ac vir una conficientes."

Scene XXVIII
69 BC

A year and a day passed by
During which I rested
In seclusion and solemn reflection.
My goddess Venus appeared to me,
And vested in me a divine capacity,
And charged me with the sacred task
Of disseminating
The Tables of the Venus Anh.

Even through that period of deep introspection,
I found strength to support my dear Caesar
During his election campaign
For the office of quaestor.
In that first year of his eligibility,
He was duly elected
And chosen to serve
As deputy to Antistius Vetus,
Provincial governor of Further Spain.
Caesar readied himself to relocate.
He was saddened to be leaving me
And his wife Cornelia,
Then pregnant with their second child.
Nonetheless
We knew it important to Caesar
And to Rome
For him to fulfil his duties,
To ensure strength of the Roman Republic
In its far western reaches.

However, before Caesar departed,
Devastation struck.
While giving birth,
Cornelia died
And their son was stillborn.
Caesar delayed his travels.

We spoke at length
For many days
And I convinced Caesar
To arrange a grand public funeral
For his beloved wife,
Even though this honour
Had never been bestowed in Rome
To such a young lady.
This plan was accepted
Because Cornelia had always upheld
The Tables of the Venus Anh
And no other Roman lady
Could have been more worthy
Of splendid ceremony.

A massive assembly of citizens witnessed
The elaborate funeral procession,
Including Roman soldiers and masked actors,
That was guided into the Forum by Caesar.
He made his way to the Rostra
To deliver a loving and passionate speech
Praising and honouring Cornelia.
I remained out of view,
Paying my respects from a distance,
Tucked away within the adoring crowd.

Scene XXIX
67 BC

Caesar departed for Further Spain
And returned to Rome
A few years later,
Having succeeded
In his administration of duties.
A rumour spread
That Caesar had returned early to Rome
Because he had suffered from seizures.
But I assumed this to be folly,
Anticipating the true reason
For Caesar's return to Rome,
That being to marry again.
Of course, I knew Caesar loved me,
And expected
Our imminent wedding announcement.
But it was not to be.

My Caesar,
My lover,
Broke to me
The news that he should wed
Pompeia, granddaughter of Sulla.
This was not for love,
But for politics,
To please the steadfast supporters of Sulla,
Including senators and many other Romans.
I pleaded with my dear Caesar
To abandon this ill-advised plan,

For I had conversed with this woman prior
And knew of her tarnished character
And ill health.
It was known
Amongst many Romans
That Pompeia
Had seduced young boys
And, even knowing she spread her disease
During sexual pleasures,
She continued her evils.
Thus, she did not uphold
The Tables of the Venus Anh,
Even though I advised her
Of her duties as a woman:
Leadership,
Showing the right way forward;
Service,
Working for the betterment of our society;
Love,
Protecting and nurturing those around us.

I also came to know
That one of her lover boys
Was Marcus Junius Brutus,
Caesar's own son.
Pompeia had seduced him
A few years prior
When he was only 15 years of age.
I knew that if Caesar
Had knowledge of this,
He would take action under temper
Against his son.
Therefore, I did not share
This knowledge with my dear Caesar.

But I told him
Of Pompeia's questionable character
And sexual addictions.
"Nonetheless", Caesar conceded,
"I must wed her
So that I can take the Republic
Another step forward.
But I shall leave vacant
Any of her desires for intimacy."

Scene XXX
67 BC

After the wedding
I remained in Caesar's home
For a number of days,
Living in my suite as I had done
Since first arriving in Rome.
In spite of that,
Pompeia would not accept this arrangement.
I also knew it best to distance myself
From that lady, so sickly and impure.
Thus, I arranged to embark on a pilgrimage
To the city of Pompeii.
There, I knew I had much work to do
In disseminating
The Tables of the Venus Anh,
For although it was a prosperous city
Of trade and commerce,
It was also a sanctuary for improprieties
Where women laid beneath
The unchecked sway of man.
In that city,
Secluded from prying eyes throughout the Forum,
All classes of people came to indulge,
From senators and wealthy merchants,
To desperate drifters and prostitutes.
The town was alive,
Lit bright as day at night.
Streets were filled with all characters,
Moving amongst the shops,

Baths, theatres, and villas.
I spent many hours each week
Talking with women and men,
Listening to their voices, their stories,
Their questions and statements.
I spoke of the
Universal and infinite rights and duties
Of women
According to the Tables of the Venus Anh.
More and more people came to listen to me,
Gathering on the steps of temples and theatres.
Some, cynical and disbelieving,
Asked how these tables could be true.

I spoke: "Look within this city
At the senators and merchants,
The patricians and the plebeians,
The women and men.
Though of diverse origins,
All rise as one, in peace,
Upon our Republic's steady foundation
That is ever strengthening
With women's influence of calming guidance.
And though a great distance is yet to be travelled,
We began our strides along the path
Towards adoption of truths
Of the Tables of the Venus Anh
In the year 195 BC
During women's first organised demonstration.
It was then we first showed
Women's collective strength,
Forcing repeal of the Oppian law,
And rejecting the regressive forces of male hegemony.
Yet it was not to prove

Woman's strength over man,
But to set the balance
Required in our achieving society.
Look at all these men who have accomplished
And see the women who support them
With leadership, service, and love.
This is possible when these women
Are afforded their security, liberty, equality.
You, all citizens, shall disseminate these
Tabulae Veneris Anh
Lest the god Vulcan turn his good fire
Against the disbelievers in this city
And lash down the fiercest rain
Of embers and ash."
I proclaimed,
And all recited:
"*Femina ac vir una conficientes.*"

Scene XXXI
65 BC

On one occasion
As I lounged in the *caldarium*
Of a bath in Pompeii,
A woman dressed in tunic and veil
Walked to the pool's edge
And prepared to submerge
In the warm and inviting waters.

I asked: "Dear lady,
Why remain in attire?"
She responded: "My husband is fearful
Of wandering eyes of others,
So enchanted by my beauty."
I replied: "If this be true,
Let your husband also cover
The mountains and the sea,
And Rome's glorious monuments,
For their inherent beauty
May also seduce and tempt any person."

I continued:
"Woman is not called upon
To surrender her liberty
To appease her mate.
This practice legitimises
Jealously, greed and fear
Harboured by insecure men.
Although they are blessed to benefit

From their wife's alluring beauty,
These men only stir
Until it is shrouded from all.
If your concealment is aimed to erase
Another man's temptation,
Rather let him look away,
And take his burden upon himself,
For the thing of beauty
Shall not bear the guilt
Of its own magnificence.
On the contrary,
The form of woman,
The embodiment of her beautiful soul,
Is to be revealed and celebrated.
And this is spoken
In the Tables of the Venus Anh,
As a universal and infinite right
Of Liberty."
The lady smiled, and asked:
"Will you unveil me, Venus Anh?"

We sat
In the water at sunset,
Our nude figures
Pressed together.
She spoke to me:
"My body a perfect treasure,
A glorious gem from the sea,
It shall not be shamed or hidden,
It is by want of me."
We embraced,
And I felt my goddess Venus amongst us.

Scene XXXII
63 BC

Marcus Licinius Crassus,
The Roman general and politician,
And political and financial supporter of Caesar,
Was the wealthiest Roman known.
He would occasionally vacation near Pompeii
At his grand villa
Placed valiantly at the top of a hill
And lavishly fitted
With Greek and Roman statues,
Grand fountains,
Vine-covered pergolas,
And a bath complex
That overlooked the sprawling valley below.
In the centre of the villa,
An eating area within the garden
Invited guests to dine outdoors.
A system of small canals
Running between the diners
Floated dishes to guests
Who could pluck the delicacy of their choosing.

Crassus was aware
Of my presence in Pompeii,
Having spoken frequently to Caesar.
One evening,
Crassus sent a Roman soldier
To deliver a message to me.
It was an invitation to a dinner party

The following evening at his villa,
Which was arranged
To celebrate Caesar's recent election
To the position of
Pontifex Maximus in Rome.

When I arrived
I met the invited guests,
Mostly senators and other Roman politicians.
I was the only woman to attend the dinner.
Crassus took me aside for a moment
In a room adjacent to the garden dining area.
He offered me pomegranate
And raised his golden wine goblet
In a toast to me:
"During this night of opportunities
You may ask anything of me.
I will ensure your desires are satisfied."

During dinner
A feast lay before us.
Fish, olives and wine.
Walnuts, figs, and almonds.
Imported exotic fruits and spices.
Even giant clams
And wild animal meat from afar.
Slaves stood by, always at the ready,
Tending to every guest's craving.

Scene XXXIII
63 BC

Following dinner, all guests were invited
To indulge in the splendid outdoor baths.
Many other guests arrived at that time,
Most being women:
Mistresses of senators,
Greek bath attendants,
Asian masseuses,
Even some high-profile prostitutes
Known to the elite in Pompeii.

The sequential pools,
Frigidarium, tepidarium, and *caldarium*
Were serene and inviting,
Perched high above the surrounding valleys
With a view of Mt. Vesuvius.
There were no divided quarters for women –
Crassus justified the liberal
Environs of his villa:
"Pompeii is a place where
We need not have the barriers
That get in our way
Throughout the rest of the Republic."
Guests lingered in the baths,
Discussing, debating, flirting.
I mingled with guests throughout the pools.
My formal introduction was unnecessary,
For all knew of the Venus Anh
And my presence inspired some lively discussions.

One rosy old man, overfilled with Retsina,
Tilted to me and whispered
In a breath saturated with Aleppo pine resin:
"I need you tonight
As all men need their muse.
Come with me, I will pleasure you
Until the sun rises over Rome…"
"Dear man," I replied,
"Although flattered,
I am for my true lover
And no other."
I prayed for the man.

Throughout that timeless night
The soothed and aroused guests
Slipped out of the baths,
And took to other parts of the vast villa
With their lovers.
Some left in groups of three or more.
I remained in quiet solitude beside a pool until sunrise
When two young men emerged from the villa.
They were Brutus and his friend
Publius Clodius Pulcher.
Brutus spoke to me:
"We invite you to join us in the villa."
I said: "It is not possible young man,
I love Caesar, your father, and no other."
Brutus looked dismayed and grasped my arm.
"I can prove differently," he replied.
I responded: "It is better if you take Julia,
Caesar's daughter. Marry her and rejoice."
Both men fretted,
And withdrew from the villa in haste.

Scene XXXIV
62 BC

In December of the following year
I returned to Rome
As invited guest
To a splendid event
At Caesar's house.
It was filled with Vestal Virgins
And distinguished ladies of patrician class,
But off limits to men.
It was the annual festival
Of the Bona Dea,
Our divinity the Good Goddess.
The festival, a secret rite,
Was conducted at the Pontifex Maximus' home
Each December.
With wine and myrtle shunned at the event,
A farrowed sow was brought as the traditional sacrifice.

I had been invited,
Despite Pompeia's reluctance,
By Caesar's mother, Aurelia
Who organised the ritual that year.
Usually, the event was arranged by
The Pontifex Maximus' wife.
However, none had confidence in Pompeia,
Unfocused as she was.

Caesar's daughter Julia attended as well.
She told me secretly

That Pompeia
Had a boy lover
Who would attend our ritual that night
In female guise.
I was sickened,
But not surprised
That she had seduced
Such a loutish boy
While adorned with
The greatest husband in Rome.

With news of an intruder,
Aurelia and I perused
All the gathered guests.
Aurelia soon found the boy
Dressed as a lady –
His male voice gave the clue,
And out the door he flew.
I saw his face
As he fled;
Publius Clodius Pulcher it was,
Without a doubt.

The event was abruptly cancelled
With all in shock
After the sacrilegious invasion.
A messenger was sent
To retrieve Caesar.
The ladies dispersed
From Caesar's home,
And I waited for his return
Outside on that cold midwinter night.

Caesar approached me,

With bewildered expression.
"What occurred to bring such an awful close
To this ritual?" he asked me.
I replied: "Caesar, you are not with a good wife.
She brought a boy lover, in guise."
Dismayed and downtrodden,
He looked at me.
I held my sacred shell.
Looking down at it,
Without words,
My expression told him –
Woman's universal and infinite duties of
Leadership,
Service,
Love...
None respected
By Pompeia.
Caesar said: "My wife
Ought not even to be under suspicion,
But she leaves no doubt
As to her treachery."
The following day
Caesar announced
His divorce.
All of Rome saddened.
I comforted Caesar
But his angst caused him much restlessness
And he decided
He must leave Rome, alone,
And venture westward again
To Spain.

Scene XXXV
61 BC

Caesar's departure
To serve as Governor of Spain
Left me in pain.
My soulmate gone,
I moved on,
South again to Pompeii.
During my travel from Rome
Along the *Via Appia*,
Surveyed years prior by my love Caesar,
I chanced upon an equestrian sport event.
Boys were riding routes around obstacles
Placed in a field.
I stopped and watched
As one boy approached me.
"Dear lady, only boys shall ride
And only men shall watch our play,"
Said the young horseman.
I replied: "I do not interfere young man,
And my travels will take me again
Soon enough."
The youth responded: "Depart with immediacy
Or our horses shall step on your head
And your place will be gotten
Into the earth."

I instructed: "Dearest young man,
The breaching of a lady's safety,
Or even such threat,

Will condemn you.
A woman's security
Is her universal and infinite right
As spoken
In the Tables of the Venus Anh.
Which great leader
Do you aspire to emulate?
The one who benefits
From his loving bond with woman?
Are his principles the truth,
Cast in stone,
Such that his achievements
Are indelible,
Or are they illusory,
Only drawn in sand
To be washed out
By the tides of veracity?
Choose your hero wisely;
His path leads you to your fate.
Consider those
Who truly liberate their followers
And achieve peace.
Femina ac vir una conficientes.

"Dismount and give me your hand," I asked.
I took my gold coin
And placed it in his palm.
"I bless you, good son.
Take this coin and let it remind you each day
That woman and man only succeed together."
The boy watched me
As I turned and continued my journey
Along Caesar's stone-steady path.

Scene XXXVI
60 BC

While in Pompeii,
I learnt of Caesar's return to Rome
From Spain.
With my thoughts of marriage
Flaming in my heart,
I hurried my return
To his Roman house.
Yet, upon arrival,
My dreams doused once again.
He explained his long-term lust
For Servilia,
Mother of Brutus.
The woman
Was Caesar's bought desire,
His prostitute.
I said to my Caesar:
"If you love her,
Display your love, in earnest."
Caesar gifted her
With a magnificent pearl
For all of Rome to see.
However, he did not propose
To marry her;
Lust was strong
But marriage for Caesar
Was an institution
Reserved for political gain,
Driven as he was

To rule Rome
Like no other man.

Caesar instead
Took to wed
Calpurnia Pisonis,
Of age 16 years.
She was daughter
Of Lucius Calpurnius Piso,
A leading contender for consulship
And a certain ally
Of Caesar's interests.
Nonetheless,
I remained resident
At Caesar's home.
Our love for each other
Continued to burn brightly.
I lit two candles
And placed them together, touching;
I prayed
That one day
Love would trump politics
And our spirits would fuse
Like ribbons of melting wax
Trickling together, melding forever.

Scene XXXVII
59 BC

Caesar was elected
As a consul of the Roman Republic.
He relished his new power
As a law maker,
A leader of the Senate,
And a commander of the army.
He had great ambitions
For Rome and himself.
One of his aims,
To pass new land bills,
Was at the top of his agenda.
But, to fully achieve his goals,
He knew he needed powerful allies.
Thus he formed a Triumvirate
With Pompey and Crassus,
A three-way alliance
Which surely secured
Mighty legislative power
For each of them.
Despite this new support,
Caesar's drive to pass the land bills
Set up stiff opposition in the Senate
And created new enemies,
Hotly contested debates,
And flaring tempers.
Even some violence.
Caesar's anger simmered.
He became impatient and more aggressive.

He had an opponent jailed temporarily.
He was in misery.
Caesar spoke to me:
"My body flashes with anger!
I should cast these fools down
With spear and sword!"
I talked with my Caesar
At length in the evenings
After bathing and dining.
"Do not harm yourself
By threatening your foes
Or giving thought to violence,
In attempts to pass these bills,
However good and just they be.
Maintain your level,
Your composure,
Your focus.
All of Rome
Will see your laws as just and right
And no senator, in the end,
Can alter the truth.
All of Rome
Will cover the naysayers
With the dark clouds and rain
Of their hypocrisy.
I love you
And all trusted Romans love you!
We see that what you do
Is for the good of the Republic."

Caesar then went forth with his work
With cooled temper
And calmed focus.
We discussed each night

His approach for the following day.
I reviewed his notes
And we concurred on strategy.
Within a short time
The true Caesar,
The calm,
The powerful,
Creative,
And wise,
Prevailed.
His bills were passed.
The extensive programme
Of land resettlement
Was proven widely popular in Rome.
Caesar thanked me:
"You have helped me settle my thoughts
And guided me as such
Through difficult times.
My dear lover,
I have achieved,
And all of Rome has gained,
Because you fulfilled your duties of
Leadership,
Service,
Love,
As spoken
In the Tables of the Venus Anh.
Femina ac vir una conficientes."

We rejoiced.
In the following days
Caesar relaxed
In soothing baths
With massages by servants.

He once again felt fresh and energised.
Blissful in the comfort of our home,
His new young wife Calpurnia and I
Pleasured our dear Caesar
While he wore his *corona civica*
For our delight.

Scene XXXVIII
59 BC

Brutus appeared at our home
On a day while Caesar attended meetings
At the senate.
Brutus spoke:
"Venus Anh,
You advised me at Pompeii
To marry Caesar's daughter.
Alas, you are my greatest desire,
Who confounds my craving,
Thwarting our rightful bond,
The one owed to me,
And as such
You sew your own blanket of plight
That you can bind yourself with."
I rebuked: "These thoughts of yours
Will not serve you well."
Brutus responded: "I will come tonight
To request of Caesar
His Julia's hand in marriage."
I said to Brutus:
"It is not your bitter medicine
To take her, though your half sister;
You shall wed, for it is just and right.
Thus, you will strengthen your alignment
With Caesar
And support all his causes."
Brutus departed
And returned to our home

Later that night
To speak with Caesar.
Brutus' engagement
To Julia was arranged.

However, not long after,
Caesar decided it prudent
To strengthen his bond with Pompey,
To further entrench his influence
In the Republic.
He thus gave his daughter to Pompey
As his new young wife.
Brutus was advised
Of annulment of his engagement to Julia.
His protesting raged, to no avail.

Days later,
Brutus spoke to me:
"What have I to do?
Failing to seduce you
Or even Caesar's daughter,
Shall I take revenge
And give back what is just
To you and Caesar?"
I replied:
"Young man, it is arranged
That you shall assist Cato, governor of Cyprus,
And you shall serve Rome
With your good work there."
Brutus,
Still enraged,
Departed
With great anger in his eyes.

Scene XXXIX
59 BC

At the conclusion
Of Caesar's year-long consulship,
The passage of the *Lex Vatinia*
Assigned him as governor
Of Cisalpine Gaul and Illyricum.
The appointment delighted Caesar.
He said to me:
"It is now for all to see
I am the greatest servant of the Republic."
In his glee,
Caesar also said in the Senate:
"I have gained my greatest desire
To the great grief of my enemies
And I will now mount on their heads."

Before Caesar departed for Gaul,
I told him: "My love,
Strive to be
The greatest servant of the Republic.
The Romans will reward you
Beyond your expectations.
Glorious triumphs to you,
My dear.
Upon your return to Rome,
All will hail Caesar."

Scene XL
54 BC

Caesar led his army
Across the whole of Gaul
With triumph over triumph,
And charged even further north,
Across a stormy channel
To a distant island
Named Britannia.

Despite the distance
So great between us,
I was compelled to send a letter
With immediacy
To my dear Caesar
To advise of the death
Of his mother Aurelia,
And also the death
Of his pregnant daughter
A short time later.
Julia had died during childbirth
Which I was attending.
The lovely lady,
Young wife of Pompey,
I held in my arms, tenderly
As she perished.
I felt as if
She was a daughter of mine.

Scene XLI
50 BC

It was unthinkable
When Caesar departed for Gaul
That he would remain there
For nine years,
Achieving more than he ever dreamt,
And more than Romans ever expected.
His myriad of triumphs
Over the entire region
From the Atlantic to the Rhine,
And from the Mediterranean to Britannia
Utterly defeated all challenging tribes,
Establishing Roman rule
And Caesar's unequivocal power
Throughout all of Gaul.
The conquest was complete.
"The whole of Gaul is conquered,"
Wrote Caesar in a note to me.
In the same note
He invited me to join him in Gaul
On the shores of the Mediterranean:
"I shall send for you my dear.
My trusted general Marcus Antonius
Will collect you at Rome
And bring you to me
At a secluded and tranquil bay
By the sea."

I was ushered

In gilded ancient chariot
By Marcus and Roman soldiers
Along the Mediterranean shoreline
Past the Gulf of Genoa
To the settlement of Nicaea.
There, Caesar and I
Savoured the soothing baths
On the hillside
Overlooking the ocean
And we lounged on the pebbly beach
While sipping wines from the Rhône valley,
Now our valley, a valley of the Romans.

I spoke to Caesar:
"A woman in Rome who drinks wine
As I do tonight can be sentenced to death.
Yet you allow me this liberty
Not afforded to other Roman women.
For that I thank you
My dear Caesar,
As I know you do it
Because you love me
And because you embrace
My rights set forth
In the Tables of the Venus Anh.
Yet all women of Rome
Deserve the rights of their men.
They yearn for equality.
They dream of achieving their rights,
Their right to vote,
To participate in politics,
To travel freely,
To have a say in whom they marry,
To speak their minds,

To drink wine.
I ask you dear Caesar,
As the greatest leader of Rome,
How can equality be achieved
By all Roman women?"

Caesar thought for some time, then said:
"Every wise man beholds the truth.
He knows when he has benefitted
And triumphed
With the support of his lady
As she fulfils her universal and infinite duties
Of the Tables of the Venus Anh.
Yet did he allow her
The corresponding rights?
If not, he the wise man
Soon corrects this imbalance
That surely limits his own potential.
Others choose to deny;
Let them take falsehood
And let them diminish themselves.
Gaul is conquered,
But our campaign
To advance our society
Never ends.
Where paternalism falls,
Civilizations rise.
When we fight the just fight,
The gods delight."

At that moment
On the pebbly beach
Caesar took my hand
And we stood together.

He spoke:
"Dearest Venus Anh,
With my successes here now achieved,
And my marriages having fulfilled
Their political purposes,
Without love,
I duly propose to you,
My true love and soulmate,
It is time
That we wed.
I can resist no longer,
And we shall go together
As we've always wished,
Forever.
Will you marry me?"
"Yes I will," I said.
And our hearts rejoiced.

Scene XLII
49 BC

I retreated back home
While Caesar remained in Gaul
To facilitate orderly transition of command there.
He intended to return to Rome
Later that year.

However,
Shortly after my return,
I received a letter from Caesar:
"My love,
I yearn for times of stability
And rule of law in our Republic,
Yet that time has not arrived.
My enemies in Rome
Who have even lured Pompey,
My great friend and ally,
Have aligned against me and
Intend to strip me of power
By any means.
I am on the road
From Ravenna to Ariminum.
I cannot return to Rome in safety,
As Pompey
Will not lay down his arms,
Even if I agree to do so.
Rome must be defended,
And I am the true defender.
Our current leaders

Do not respect the Republic,
Do not respect the law.
They have even stripped the rights
Of the tribunes of the people,
Ignoring their right to veto.
I have decided
I must pass from Gaul
Into Roman territory
Across the Rubicon
With my Thirteenth Legion and cavalry.
This surely will set off
A great battle in Rome.
But my choices are none.
And I pray
For the best outcome for the Republic,
For my warriors, for myself
And for you, my love.
To achieve this,
I must defend my *dignitas*,
With no expense spared."

I returned a letter
To Caesar with haste:
"Dearest Caesar, I pray with you
And support your defence
Of our Republic.
I am with you in spirit.
No chance have I
To save you
But I support you with my love."

Caesar told me years later
That as he led his army
To the Rubicon

He stopped and pondered
Before crossing,
Knowing his action
Would cause a Roman civil war.
He rested with his army
Near the riverbank
For the evening,
And woke the next morning
To the sight of my image
Appearing before him
As a figure
At the edge of the river,
Holding the sacred shell
To my chest.
Caesar and his army
Then followed me
Across the Rubicon
As I led them
With my sacred dagger raised.
We thrust onward
With great resolve
To defend Caesar,
To defend Rome.

As we marched together,
Caesar heard me say:
"The die is cast."
And Caesar replied to me:
"Yes my love,
The die is cast."

Scene XLIII
49 BC

Due to anticipated strife in Rome,
Calpurnia and I
Retreated to a villa in Pompeii,
One secretly owned by Caesar
And guarded by soldiers.
We comforted each other
And prayed for Caesar,
Our lover.
Caesar wrote to me,
Asking for my support and
Leadership,
Service,
Love.
I wrote to Caesar:
"My love,
You should meet Pompey
Who is leading opposition to you.
Meet face-to-face,
And come to terms.
You are the greatest leader,
Dear Caesar,
And you shall lead to the solution."

And so Caesar invited Pompey
To meet with him privately
Near Ariminum.
Pompey responded to Caesar:
"We shall meet

Not at Ariminum,
But rather at the Senate.
And only after
You withdraw your army
Back to Gaul."

Caesar wrote to me afterwards:
"My dear Venus Anh,
Pompey has refused my offer
And countered with the untenable,
Thus he secures his own demise;
I now advance
To take all of Rome
Under my dominion."

Scene XLIV
49 BC

Even with only a fraction
Of his army available to him,
Caesar advanced efficiently
Through the length
Of the Italian peninsula
From Ariminum
All the way to Brundisium.
Caesar wrote to me: "We
The defenders of the Republic
Have already, within two months,
Forced Pompey's thin forces
To retreat to the end of land
And across the Adriatic channel
To Greece.
My recent invitations
To meet face-to-face
With Pompey
Were again denied
By this stubborn man.
The folly of his ways
Must surely have set in
Amongst he and his followers.
As we re-establish proper Roman rule
Along the whole length of Italy,
I offer civility and clemency
To those we defeat.
Thus, we continue to attract support
Of the locals

Wherever we go.
We even convince
Some of the captured Pompeians
To join our good cause,
As they see that we
Are the true defenders of the Republic.
The brilliance of our civilised approach
Undoubtedly strengthens our side.
My impetus for this approach,
Venus Anh,
Is your kind guidance to me,
As you have given me over the years,
To show restraint and compassion,
And focus on the result,
Not flamboyant display
Of force or victory.
I have been rewarded in doing so
With our continued success.
Therefore, I praise you.
Thanks be to you, Venus Anh."

Scene XLV
49 BC

At long last,
After nearly a decade of travels,
My dear Caesar
Returned to Rome.
Calpurnia and I
Welcomed him
With adoring love.
Caesar spoke to me privately:
"Venus Anh,
As we promised each other
In Gaul,
We shall wed.
You are my one true love,
My only love.
You must know
My courting
Of all others
Was for no purpose
Other than to strengthen my position
As the defender of the Republic,
For the good of Rome."

But then
As Caesar continued speaking,
My heart broke
Once again
With news
Of his imminent departure.

He said: "I shall
Return to wed you
In the most glorious ceremony,
One like never before
Witnessed in Rome.
But now, with haste,
I must completely subdue
All rebelling Pompeians,
First in Spain,
Then in Greece,
And wherever they flee afterward.
For this great Republic,
I defend to the end.
And when all is settled,
I will return to Rome,
To you, my love."

Scene XLVI
47 BC

By the middle of 47 BC
Caesar wrote to me:
"My dear Venus Anh,
We have achieved our defence
Of the Republic
With victories in Spain,
Then in Greece,
Where we pushed Pompey
And his army
To flee to Egypt.
Our great force has prevailed.
But in sadness,
Pompey suffered a cruel execution
At the hands of the Egyptians
Upon his arrival there.
For me, it was devastating
As I never cheered at the thought
Of killing Pompey,
My great mentor,
And a great leader of Rome,
But rather,
I sought only his respect
Which, in the end,
He did not pay me."

Caesar's letter continued:
"I followed Pompey
To Egypt

Before learning
Of his demise.
Once there,
I campaigned to secure the Egyptian throne
For the most worthy
Of royal figures,
One who will be supportive of Rome,
She being Cleopatra VII.
This is accomplished,
And as all know
Across the Roman Republic,
From east to west,
And north to south,
I say to you,
Veni,
Vidi,
Vici –
I came,
I saw,
I conquered.
And now,
My dear Venus Anh,
I am returning to Rome,
To you, my love."

Scene XLVII
47 BC

Caesar returned to Rome
And told me: "The civil war
Has not yet been extinguished,
As Pompeian forces in Africa
Have joined the army of,
And are being led by,
King Juba I of Numidia.
They are loyal to Pompey
And threaten Rome.
It is a disgrace that Roman soldiers
Fight under a foreign leader.
I must lead my army now
To defeat this remaining thorn."
"My dear Caesar," I said,
"When will these wars ever end?
I beg you to do as you must
To defend the Republic,
But not a sword more,
Lest perpetual bloodshed.
Our Republic must settle in peace."
Caesar replied: "Do not fear,
I will crush
The African resistance
With haste."

Scene XLVIII
47 BC

With Caesar gone to Africa,
I was left alone again in Rome
With his wife Calpurnia.

I received a letter from Caesar:
"My Dear Venus Anh,
I see now
More than ever
The need for our society
To uphold
The Tables of the Venus Anh.
The peoples here in Africa,
Blanketed in paternalism
And despotism
Beyond anything seen in Rome,
Have all hopes smothered.
In this society
At the hands of King Juba I,
To be sure,
Prosperity and enlightenment are implausible.
This system, which casts women aside
And retains all wealth solely for the monarch,
Grips these lands that tumult and burn.
Behold the citizens here
Who oppose this system
And who dare to see the truth,
They see the glory of our Republic,
And will pivot to Rome.

They will risk life and limb
At high seas on the Mediterranean
As they struggle to reach our *magnifica societas*.
Even more so when I alone rule Rome
And enact the Tables of the Venus Anh.
The warlords who remain here
And steadfastly follow this false system
Are in denial
And seek to take down Rome
In their jealousy of its successes.
They strain to conceal the reality
Of our superiority due to our virtues.
These naysayers,
Fail mightily they will."

I rejoiced in Caesar's affirmation
Of the truths
In the Tables of the Venus Anh
And my thoughts
Of Caesar's return
Consumed me
During many sleepless nights.
With my anticipation
Of our wedding,
To seal the bond of our hearts so pure,
I could find no way to endure
The waiting that burnt to my core.

Scene XLIX
47 BC

Brutus arrived one day at our home,
Unexpectedly.
He spoke to me: "Venus Anh,
I opposed Caesar's invasion
From across the Rubicon
And joined Pompey's side in Greece.
Upon our defeat there, I expected to die
At the hands of my father.
But he conveyed such great clemency
By pardoning me.
As a loving father,
I know he will support me
When I ask for your hand in marriage.
And this should see no obstacle,
As Caesar has also wed Cleopatra VII,
The Greek Macedonian queen of Egypt,
Who has already given birth to his child."
In disbelief I proclaimed:
"Stop these rumours at once!
I know of your desire for me,
But selfish intent and harmful tales
Will not bring us closer.
Leave this house now and only return
When Caesar is present
To hear your accounts."
Brutus, in anger,
Turned and departed.

Scene L
46 BC

Caesar returned to Rome
In July 46 BC,
Victorious
And an undeniable hero.
He was granted
Dictatorship of the Republic
For a ten-year period.
Splendid celebrations took place for 40 days,
An unprecedented recognition
For any Roman leader.
Caesar spoke to me:
"These celebrations
And the joy of Roman citizens
Will soon be eclipsed
When we announce
Our wedding plan,
As much a royal event
As can be had in Rome."
My heart was lit
With a bright flame,
Fuelled with love
And anticipation.
I replied to Caesar: "Yes,
Our souls will bond
For all to see
In Rome's royal wedding."

Scene LI
45 BC

The celebrations for Caesar
Had only just finished
When an uprising in Spain
Again threatened cohesion
In our Roman Republic.
"My dear Venus Anh," Caesar said to me,
"I have no choice but to preserve
All that we have fought for
And all that we have gained.
I must quell this threat at once,
But my promise
Is to return to you this year
And marry you."
Although I had much faith
In all that my Caesar told me,
I could not contain my disappointment,
And wept in his arms.

Caesar departed for Spain
With his army
And in swift and convincing manner,
By spring of 45 BC,
He had achieved
Yet another convincing military victory.
During his absence
I was awoken one night
By a voice.
My goddess Venus

Appeared before me
And spoke:
"Your wedding day
Shall be 21 April.
This is a sacred day
For you
And for Rome."
With insufficient time
To prepare for the wedding
In April of that year,
Our wedding date was set
For the following spring,
On 21 April 44 BC.
A sacred day
To be celebrated
Forever after.

Scene LII
44 BC

It was necessary
For Caesar and I
To keep our wedding plans
Secret from all
Until one month before the ceremony.
Caesar wished this approach,
As he explained to me:
"During my absence from Rome,
Many administrative requirements
Have remained incomplete
And mishandled
To the detriment of our citizens.
I wish to do my work
In a focused manner
Without a distraction to all of Rome,
Which surely the news of our wedding
Will be, like no other."
Not even Caesar's wife Calpurnia
Knew of the wedding plans,
Even though we shared a bed
And we shared our Caesar.

One morning in March
I disclosed the news to her:
"My dearest Calpurnia,
Your love for Caesar
Is commendable and steady.
Please understand,

It is the wish of our goddess Venus
That I shall wed Caesar,
As a divine event,
A royal bonding.
It is the calling of Rome
That sets us together."
Expressions of disillusionment
Set upon her face.

That night,
In our bed
Calpurnia awoke me
With such a fright.
"I fear for Caesar," she said.
"Fear not, he will be cared for
Like no other," I said.
"No, my dear," said Calpurnia,
"I saw harm to him, in my dream.
He lay slain on top of me."

Scene LIII
44 BC

The following day,
On the Ides of March,
Brutus arrived at our home,
Frantically bashing the door.
"What horrible news!" he shouted at me.
"Mother Servilia has told me
Of your plan to wed my father!"
"Yes Brutus, it is true," I said.
Brutus exclaimed: "First Julia
Was promised to me, then ripped away.
Now this deceit, it cannot happen!
I am your rightful husband!
How many rewards
Does Caesar require?"
I replied:
"Goddess Venus
Imparts this wish
For all of Rome,
A royal gift.
Our marriage casts
A guiding ray,
The light of life
For all who pray.
Femina ac vir una conficientes."

With that,
Brutus struck me to the floor
And charged inside.

"Caesar will pay
The greatest price
For this injustice!"
He shouted
As he marched back outside
As quickly as he had entered.
Calpurnia tended to me,
Lifting me into a chair.
As I sat and recovered,
I saw that my sacred dagger
Was not beside the chair
Where I always kept it.

Scene LIV
44 BC

"My nightmare!
It must not materialize!" cried Calpurnia.
We ran towards Pompey's Theatre
Where Caesar was in the senate session.
Guards halted us
Outside a set of massive wood doors.
"Brutus must be stopped!" I demanded.
The guards said nothing,
But stepped aside.
Calpurnia and I
Heaved on one of the doors
To open it just enough
For us to burst inside,
Only to see
Our dear Caesar
Lying slain on the floor.

The sacred sword fashioned by Mother Anh,
Razor-sharp steel so made to protect me,
Plunged deep within the body of my man,
My lover so grand and Rome's king to be.
The divine dagger I pulled out of him
And looked up above for angels to aid,
But none appeared and the room seemed to dim.
In deafening silence my Caesar laid
In blood-bath, surrounded by men whose souls
Had been poisoned in greed and jealousy.

I peered above
And beckoned my goddess Venus:
"For what cause, this toll?
Is this sword only to turn against me?"
She appeared before me, her voice like song:
"Your sword casts its prey to where they belong."

Scene LV
44 BC

Four ladies stood
On the steps
Of the Temple of Jupiter
And I spoke to them:
"The Tables of the Venus Anh
Proscribe woman's
Universal and infinite rights of
Security,
Liberty,
Equality,
And woman's
Universal and infinite duties of
Leadership,
Service,
Love.
Go forth my ladies
And spread these truths
To all women and men
And live in peace."
We all recited:
"*Femina ac vir una conficientes.*"

One lady said to me:
"Someone awaits you!
Come with us to the river."
The ladies walked with me
From the Forum
To the Tiber, then across the river

On the recently constructed arch bridge
To a small boat
Moored at the river island.
The ladies assisted me to sit comfortably
In the trusty vessel
As I carried my sacred shell
And my dagger for protection.
I alone drifted quietly down the river
To its terminus where it's consumed
By the vast sea,
At which point
I landed at the shore
And walked up the sandy beach
With lush trees beside.
After some time
I sat in warm sunlight,
Against a large rock,
And fell into a dreamy sleep.

I awoke to the sound
Of a lovely female voice:
"Hello."
The voice of my goddess Venus,
Goddess of love.
Goddess of beauty and sex,
Of fertility and desire,
Of prosperity and victory.
My goddess,
From whom my Caesar descended.
She asked: "What have you learnt
Of woman and the world?"

As the sun set,
Blanketing the beach at Ostia

In an orange glow,
We walked together
Into the evening breeze
Towards the sea,
The endless sea,
Dancing with limitless
Glittering sparkles.
"Can you hear the wind blow?" asked my goddess.
"Yes, I can hear the wind blow," I replied.
"Can you see the waves, where they go?" she asked.
"Yes, I see the waves," I replied.
I sunk my dagger's blade deep into the sand.
Four angels appeared above us.
And so the Tables of the Venus Anh
May spread to every land,
To every woman and man,
I held my shell
To my chest,
And walked with my goddess Venus
Into the sea.

Acknowledgements and References

The author thanks the following people who made valuable contributions to this epic: Megan Falconer Ward, Doctoral Student, Dept. of Greek & Roman Studies, The University of Calgary, Canada; Claire Wingfield, Editor, Dunfermline, Fife, UK; Dr. David Butterfield, Faculty of Classics, The University of Cambridge, UK.

The author has reviewed the following publications and resources during the composition of this epic:

BBC (2014), *Greek Methods of Diagnosis and Treatment*, www.bbc.co.uk/schools/gcsebitesize/history/shp/ancient/g reekmethodsrev1.shtml

Beard, M. (2015), *SPQR, A History of Ancient Rome*, London, Profile Books Ltd.

Cavazzi, F. (2012), *The Illustrated History of the Roman Empire*, www.roman-empire.net/founding/found-index.html

Cowell, F.R. (1961), *Life in Ancient Rome*, New York, Penguin Group.

D'Ambra, E. (2007), *Roman Women*, New York, Cambridge University Press.

D'Amato, R. and Sumner, G. (2009), *Arms and Armour of the Imperial Roman Soldier*, Yorkshire, Frontline Books.

Goldsworthy, A. (2006), *Caesar, Life of a Colossus*, New Haven and London, Yale University Press.

Mason, M.K. (2016), *Ancient Roman Women: A Look at Their Lives*, www.moyak.com/papers/roman-women.html

Scheidel W. (2009), *Rome and China: Comparative Perspectives on Ancient World Empires*, Oxford University Press.

Wikipedia (2016), *Han Dynasty*, https://en.wikipedia.org/wiki/Han_dynasty

The Tables of the Venus Anh

Woman's universal and infinite rights of

SECURITY

LIBERTY

EQUALITY

And woman's universal and infinite duties of

LEADERSHIP

SERVICE

LOVE